The Day I Forgot to Wash My HANDS

illustrated by Andy Elkerton

SCHOLASTIC INC.

Written by Anna W. Bardaus. Illustrated by Andy Elkerton. Designed by Marcel Dojny.

Page 32 © Roi and Roi/Shutterstock

ISBN-13: 978-1-338-28414-0
ISBN-10: 1-338-28414-2

6 7 8 9 10   40   27 26 25 24 23 22 21

Scholastic Inc., 557 Broadway, New York, NY 10012

This is the story of how my hands grew
to such a **gargantuan** size
that I could not fit through my own bathroom door...
imagine my **shock** and **surprise!**

You see, one **fine** day—
a long week ago—
in the faraway land of my yard,

I did something that, well...I **shouldn't** have done.
And the lesson it taught me was hard.

It started with **jam**, so sticky and tart,
on a sandwich of crumbly bread,
and what I did **next** might leave you aghast.
I'm not sure just what went through my head.

For after **one** game,
I moved on to the next—

it continued that way
the **whole day!**

"Sticky things stick." Or so goes the claim.
I found out that day, it is **true!**
A truer thing, actually, never was told!
Yes, **stick** is what sticky things do!

At first, it was **jam**. No great big deal, right?
Or so I thought, as you all know.
But stick a **jam hand** way down in the **sand**...
and you'll see how the problem can **grow**.

After the sand,
I monkeyed with **leaves**,

some
pinecones,

and cut-grass
confetti.

Then I sat in the sun
making **masterful** art—

'til I found I was getting
quite **sweaty**.

Feeling a **thirst**, I headed inside—
after wrestling open the **door**—

and all of a sudden, things got very **hairy**,
as I passed behind Grandpa **Abnor**.

Try as I might, I could not shake it **loose**!
And the effort? It cost me quite **dearly.**

For, in the hubbub, I regrettably pet
our beloved pet toy poodle, Shearly.

If you can believe,
from there it got **worse:**

I twirled into
a **cereal box...**

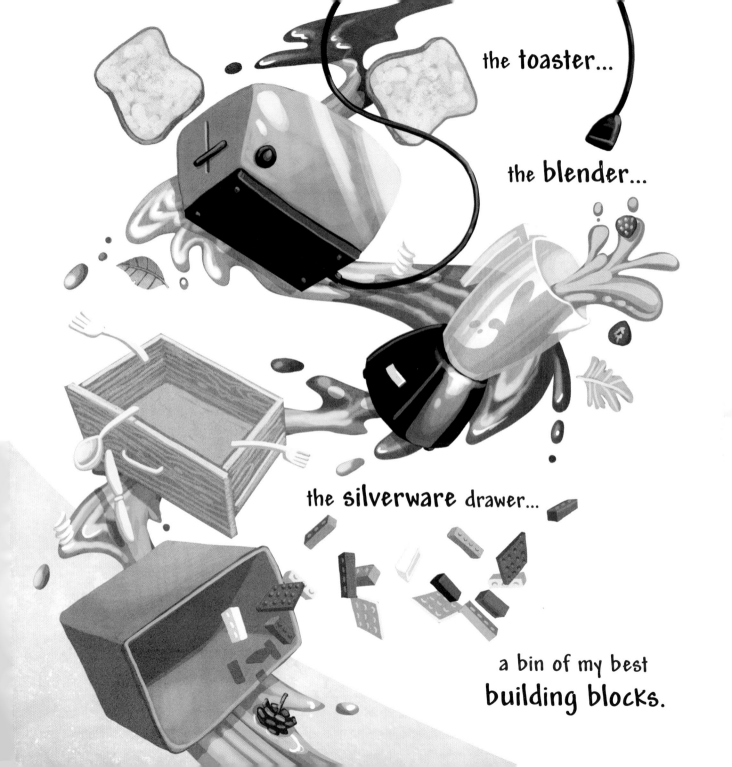

the toaster...

the blender...

the silverware drawer...

a bin of my best building blocks.

I tried to **slow** down, to stop the mad rush
of things that were **accumulating,**
but my hands grew a **gravity field** all their own,
and the madness was **accelerating!**

If you've ever been inside a **tornado booth**,
then you know just how **thrown** I was feeling,
as my hands spun **around** me at satellite speed.
The centrifugal force left me **reeling!**

Finally, **thanks be!**, they came to a rest.
There simply was **no** room for more!
I stood panting and feeling so **very** distressed,
with my hands sprawled out, **huge**, on the floor.

But in the same breath, I heard Mom head my way
and I thought, "I cannot let her see me!"
So I tugged and I lugged my vast hands down the hall,
in hopes I could wash them and be free.

Alas, as you know, it was **not** meant to be.
For, though I got near to the door
and saw my escape just inches inside,
I could drag my hands closer no more.

I'd left in my wake a wide trail to the crime,
which my mother discovered with ease.
The look on her face was not short of the worst,
most foreboding, wild brand of displeased.

But I knew that was truly **untrue.**
I knew it as well as I know my own name...
and I'd hazard to guess, so do **you.**

You see, if I'd just gone and **washed off** my hands,
the shenanigans would have stopped there.

(But so then would the tale
of this woeful affair,
and I'd not have
a story to share!)

For better or worse, I did what I did.
In the end, it was water that saved me
(and a whole box of soap, and a mean, hearty scrub,
for that's what it took to deglaze me).

Now...for the time being, I'm not **touching** jam.
But just so the world understands:

If I **ever** eat spread on crumbly bread,
we all know I'll be washing my hands.

Wacky Words
to Know

Here are some words from the book that might be new to you. See if you can find them in the story!

gargantuan: really, really, really, really big *p. 3*

aghast: shocked and horrified *p. 6*

hubbub: a noisy situation *p. 17*

accelerating: getting faster and faster *p. 20*

centrifugal force: the strong outward-pulling feeling you get when you spin, such as on a merry-go-round *p. 21*

reeling: feeling dizzy and staggering *p. 21*

foreboding: the feeling that something not good is about to happen *p. 25*

shenanigans: mischievous or funny happenings *p. 27*

woeful: pitifully bad *p. 27*

HANDY Hygiene Tips

Handwashing prevents more than shenanigans! Clean hands are key to whole-body health. Talk with your child about:

- **Germs!** These tiny, almost invisible things can make us sick. We pick them up everywhere, from everything we touch. Handwashing is your first defense against these creepy crawlies!

- **Soap and water!** Washing your hands is easy:

 ❶ Wet them.

 ❷ Apply soap.

 ❸ Scrub.

 ❹ Rinse.

 ❺ Dry!

STORY-TIME Tips

⭐ Rhymes can be super silly fun. As you read this book together, look for rhyming words on each page (such as p. 3 *size; surprise*). Now, think together of your own words to add. (*Size...surprise...disguise...french fries!*)

⭐ Imagine together that you're eating your favorite food. Tell your own hilarious, silly story about what would happen if you didn't wash your hands after.

Rhyming, rhythmic stories like this one can be tricky to read aloud. Don't let that faze you! The more you do it, the easier it will be. Start slowly, take your time, and enjoy.